Spot's Treasure Hunt

Eric Hill

G.P.Putnam's Sons • New York

Spot was playing in the garden with
his friends Tom, Helen and Steve.
"My dad has a new game for us to play,"
Spot said.

Just then, Spot's dad came into the garden. "Are you ready to play my new game?" he asked.

"Yes, we're ready!" everyone shouted. "It's a treasure hunt," Spot's dad said. "I've hidden six things in the garden for you to find. Here are six clues to help you."

1. It has a face and two hands
2. It is red and full of air
3. It is one of a pair
4. It can open and close
5. It is round and bouncy
6. It is small and shiny

Spot and his friends looked at the list of clues.

"What has a face and two hands?" Helen asked. Steve laughed. "I've got a face and two hands!" "Yes," Helen said, "and I can open and close my eyes, but we're not hiding."

Helen went to the flower bed. "I'm sure there'll be something in here." "Maybe," the snail said.

Tom looked behind some sacks.
"Hello," a small voice said.

"Shh," Spot said. "I can hear a ticking sound." It seemed to be coming from this flowerpot.

"I don't think so," Spot said.

"Then I've found something," Tom said.
"What is one of a pair? One shoe!
I like this game."

"Well done!" Helen said.
"I hope I find something soon."

"I'll help you," Spot said. "Let's look in
the cabbage patch."

Steve saw something red up in the
apple tree.
It was much too big to be an apple.

Steve laughed.
"What's red and full of air?
A balloon!"
"Only three more to find," Tom
said. "We're doing well."

"I'll look in the shed," Helen said.

"Hello, Helen, still looking?" Spot's dad asked.
"Yes," Helen said, "and I haven't found one thing."
"Don't give up yet," Spot's dad said.
"No, I won't," Helen said.

"I've found one!" Helen shouted. "What's round and bouncy? A ball!"
"Good for you," Tom said. "Only two more to find now."

Spot and Steve peeked behind a rock
by the pond.
"This looks interesting," Spot said.

"What can open and close? A box!"
Spot tried to open the box but it was locked.
"Well, this *is* a clue, but only if we
find the key."

"I found a key," a bird said. "Maybe it's the one you are looking for."

"Thank you," Spot said. "That's the last clue!"
"Yes!" Steve said. "What's small and shiny?
A key!" Spot put the key in the lock and turned it. Click!

"Gold coins!" Spot said.
"And a note," Steve said.
Helen took a coin and unwrapped it.
"Mmm, *chocolate* coins! Yummy!"
Spot read the note.
"Great! Dad is taking all of us to
the fair tomorrow!"